SILLY LILLY

AND THE FOUR SEASONS

A TOON BOOK BY
Agnès Rosenstiehl

TOON BOOKS IS AN IMPRINT OF CANDLEWICK PRESS

for Roro

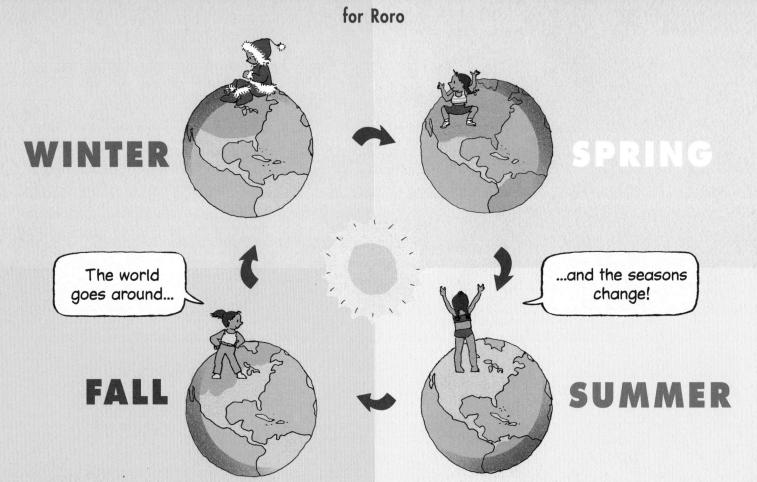

WINTER

SPRING

The world goes around...

...and the seasons change!

FALL

SUMMER

A TOON Book™ © 2008 RAW Junior, LLC, 27 Greene Street, New York, NY 10013. TOON Books® is an imprint of Candlewick Press, 99 Dover Street, Somerville, MA 02144. No part of this book may be used or reproduced in any manner whatsoever without written permission except in the case of brief quotations embodied in critical articles and reviews. TOON Books®, LITTLE LIT® and TOON Into Reading!™ are trademarks of RAW Junior, LLC. All rights reserved. Library of Congress Control number 2007941869. ISBN: 978-0-9799238-1-4 (hardcover) Printed in Dongguan, Guangdong, China by Toppan Leefung   13 14 15 16 17 18 TPN 10 9 8 7 6 5 4 3 2 1   ISBN: 978-1-935179-23-8 (paperback)

WWW.TOON-BOOKS.COM

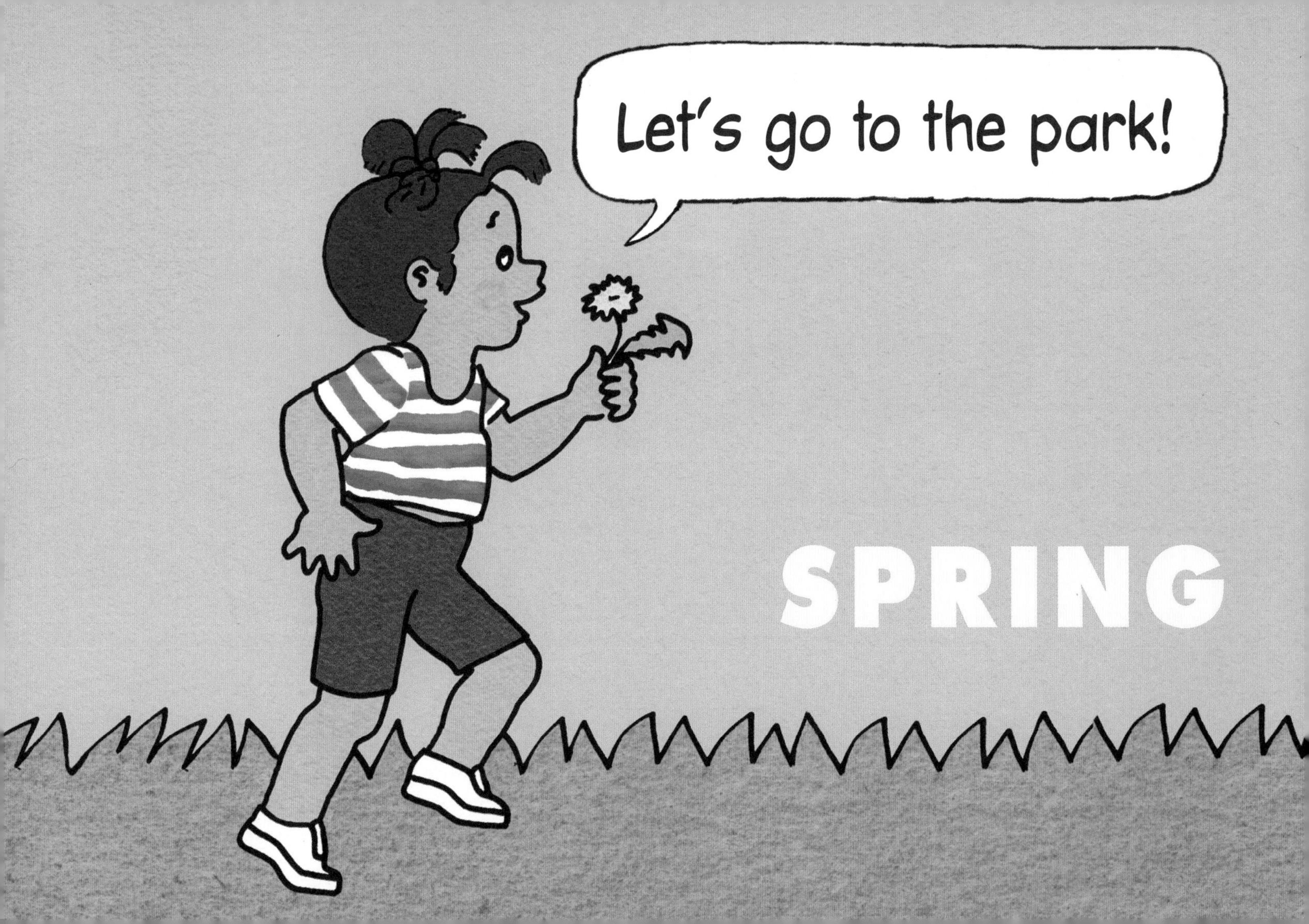
Let's go to the park!
SPRING

SILLY LILLY

AT THE PARK

There is so much to do at the park!

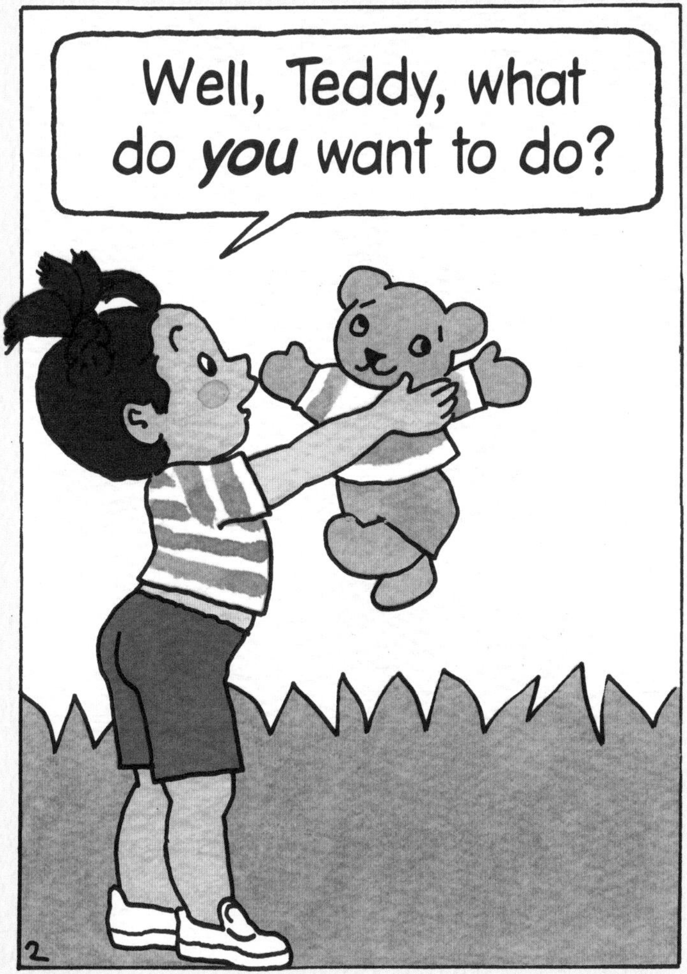
Well, Teddy, what do *you* want to do?
2

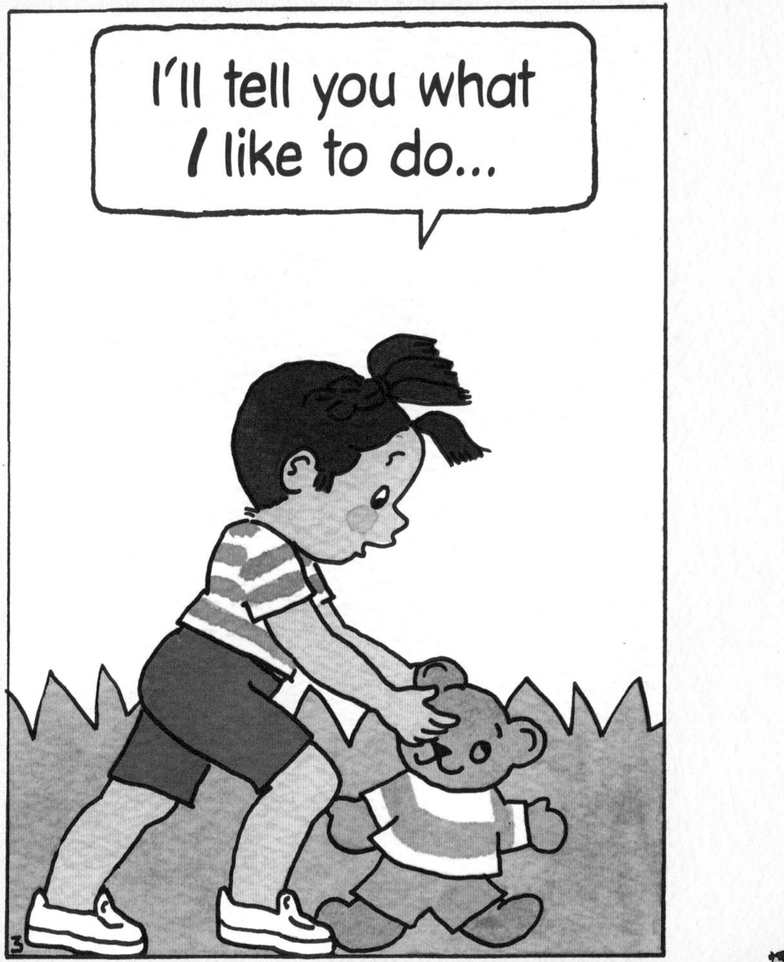
I'll tell you what *I* like to do...
3

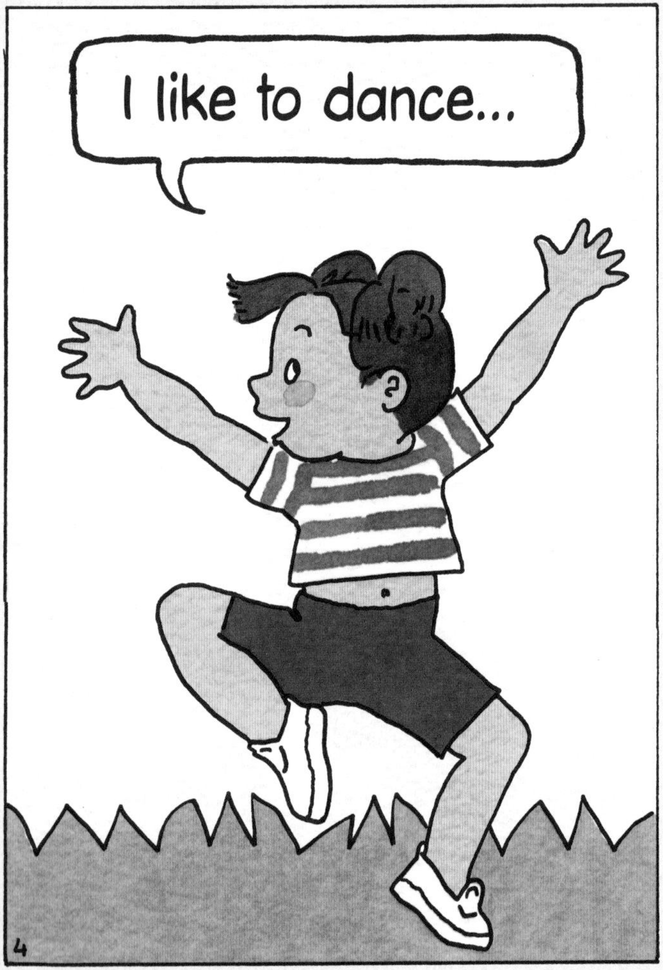
I like to dance...
4

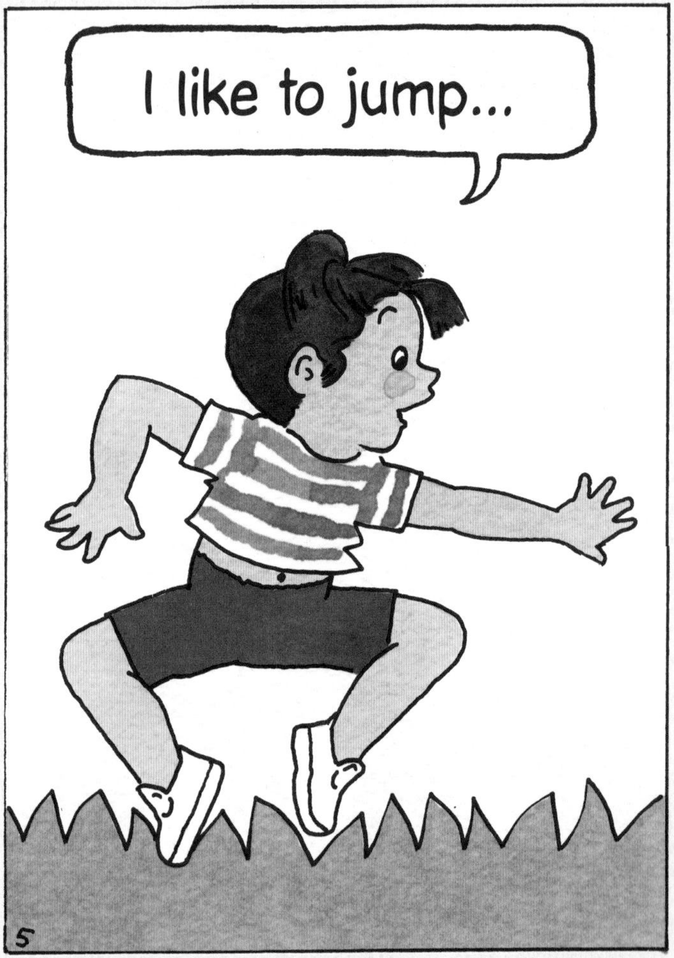
I like to jump...
5

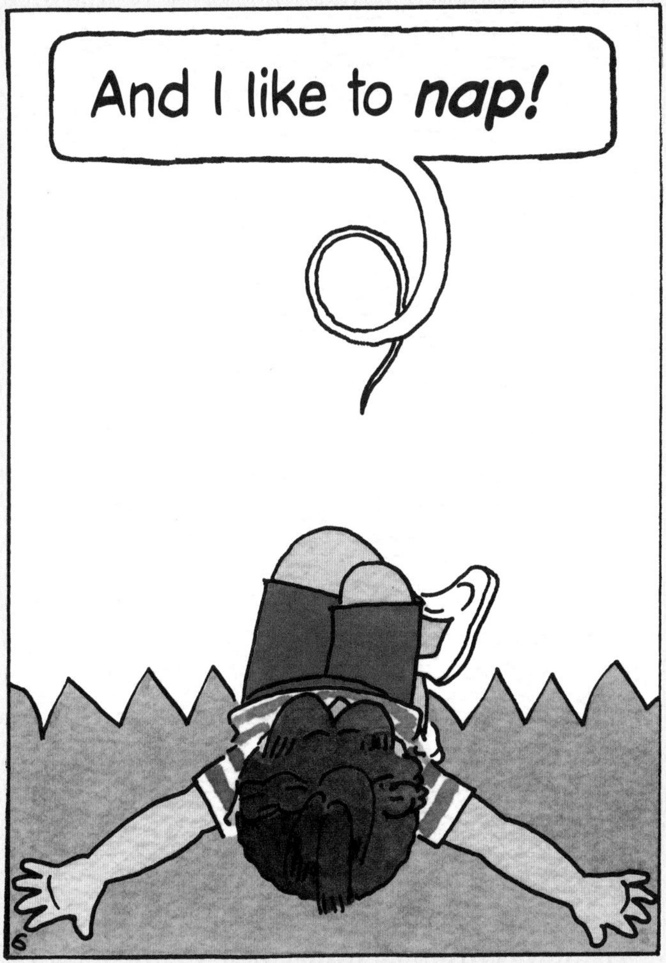
And I like to ***nap!***

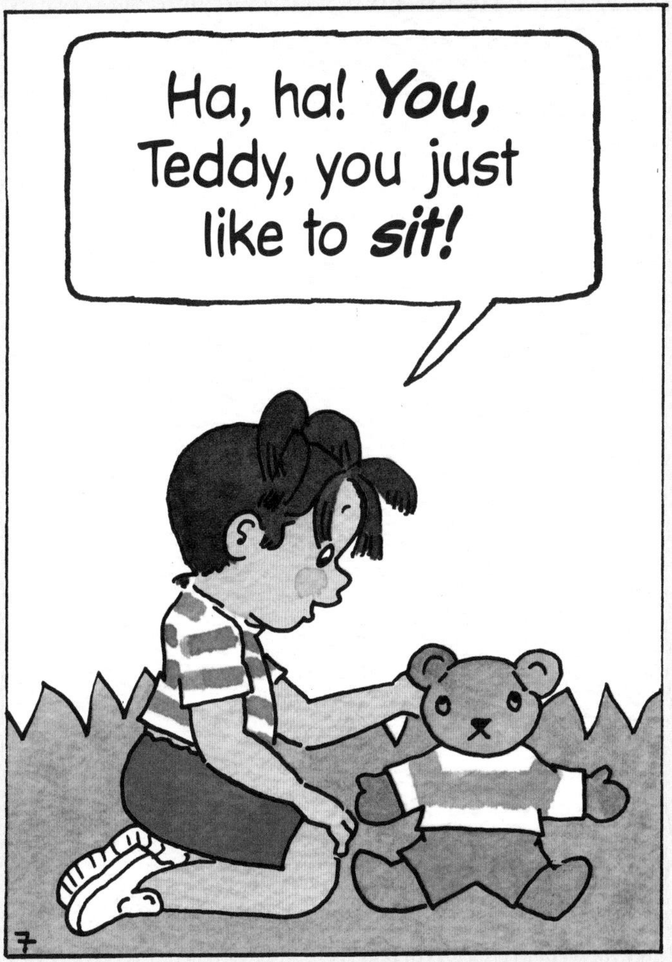
Ha, ha! ***You,*** Teddy, you just like to ***sit!***

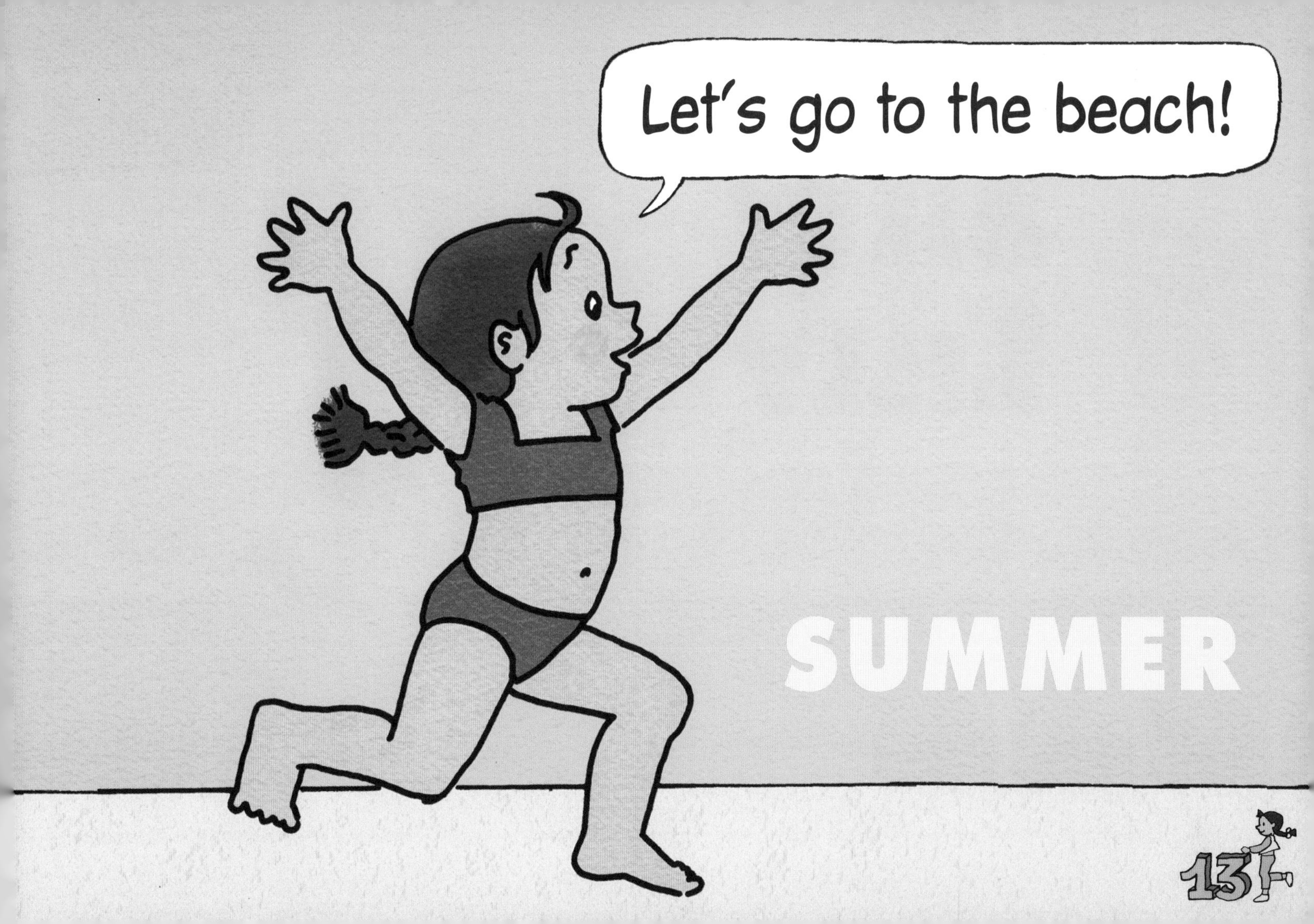
Let's go to the beach!
SUMMER

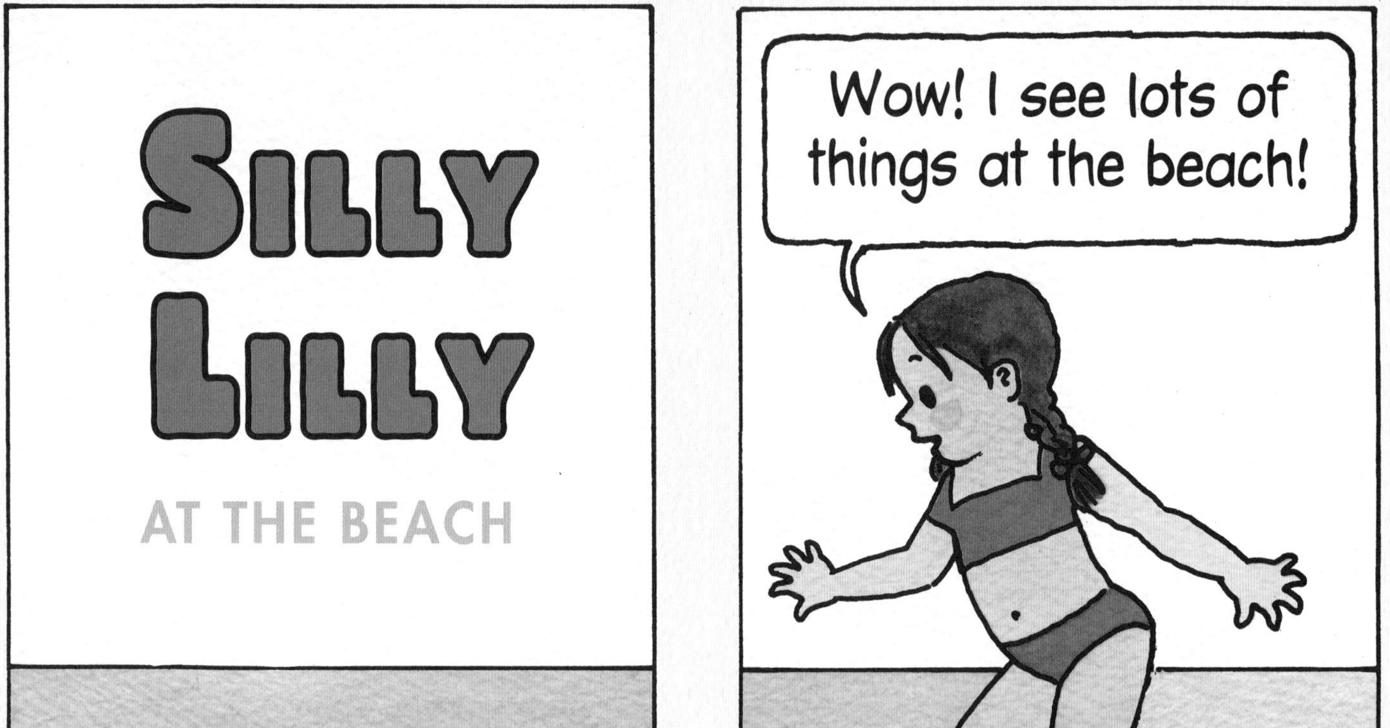
SILLY LILLY
AT THE BEACH
Wow! I see lots of things at the beach!

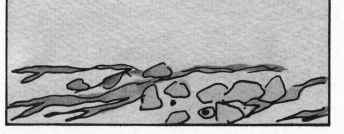

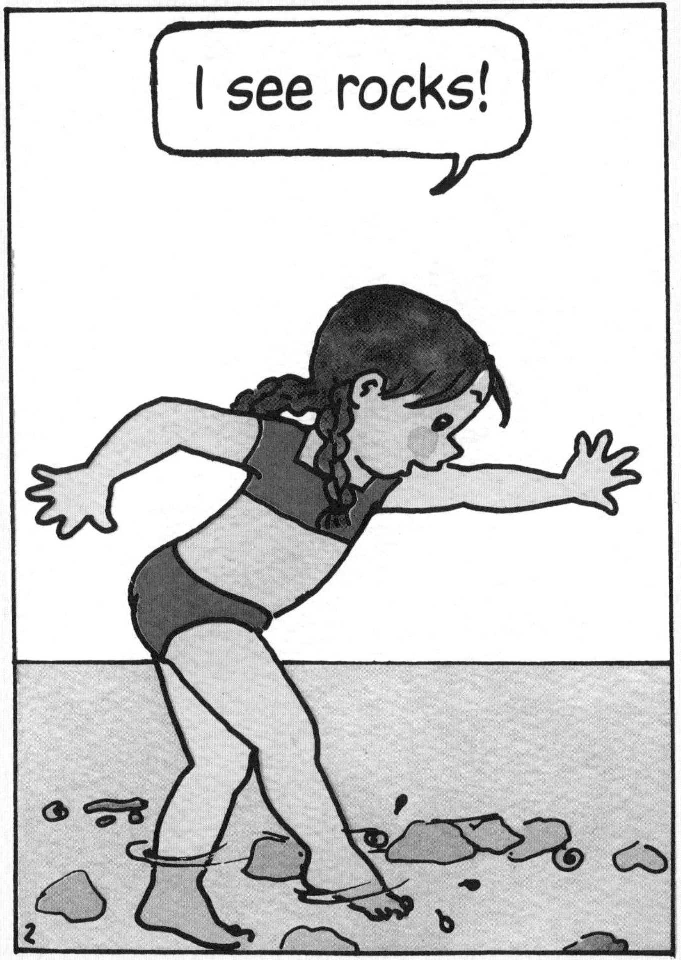
I see rocks!

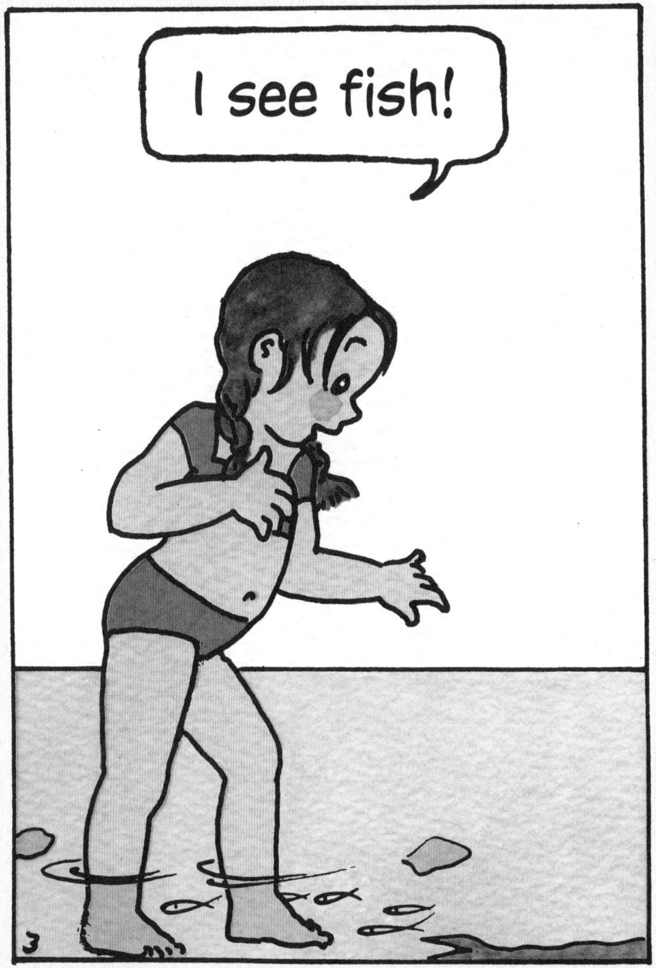
I see fish!

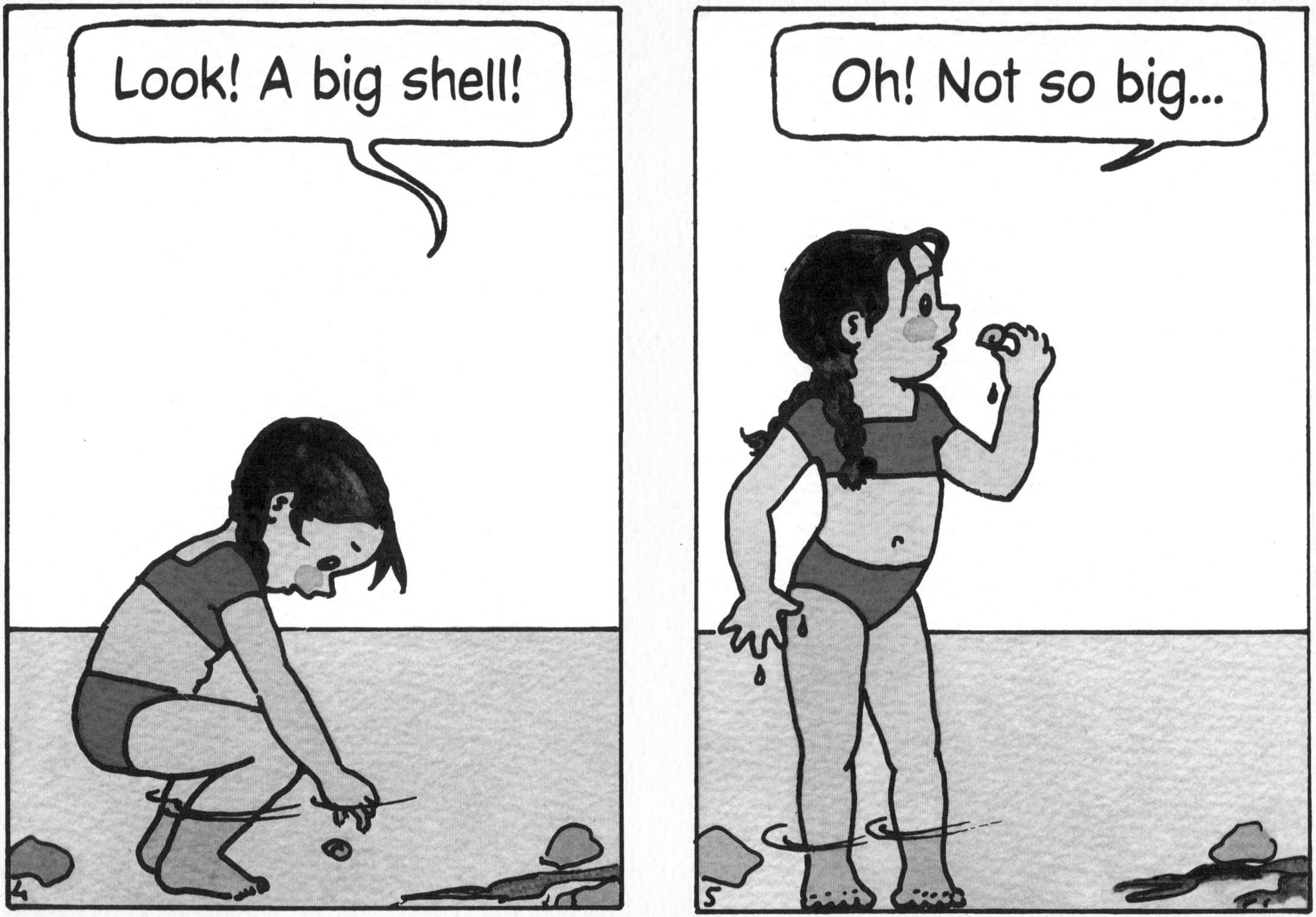
Look! A big shell!
Oh! Not so big...

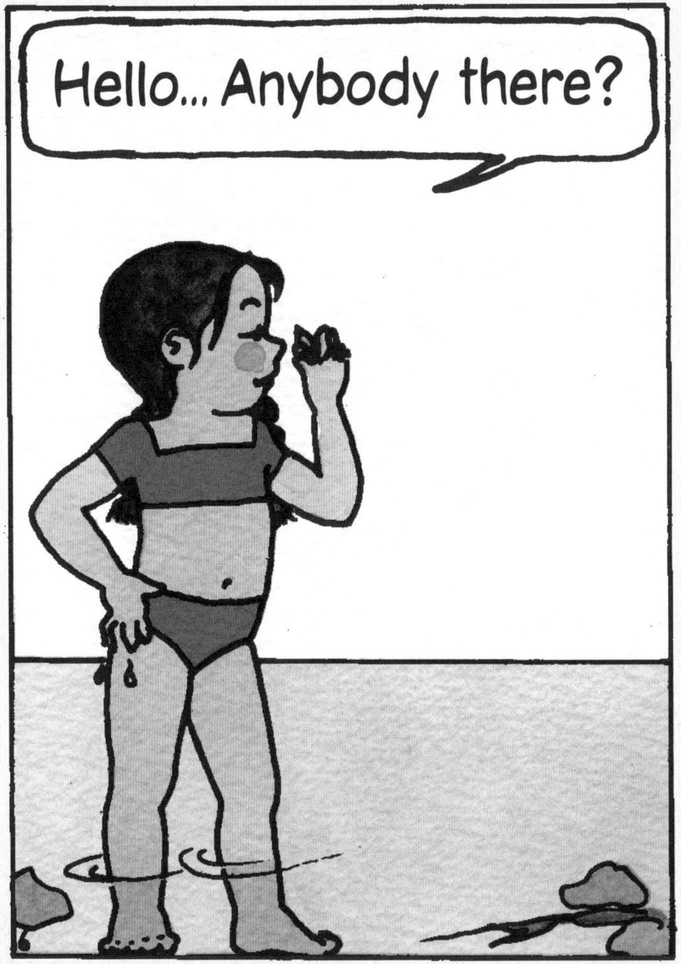
Hello... Anybody there?

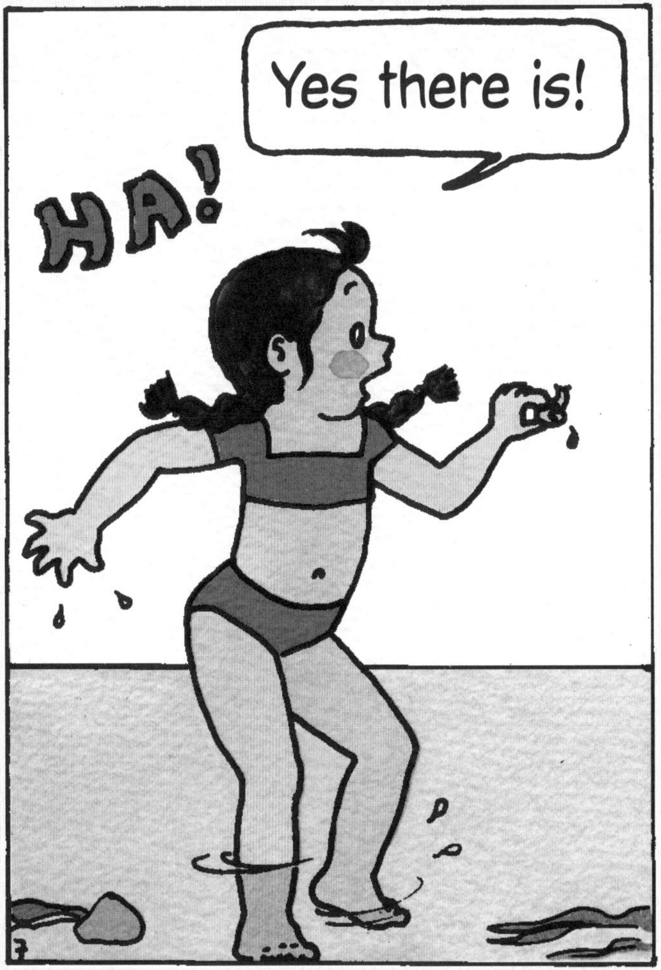
Yes there is!
HA!

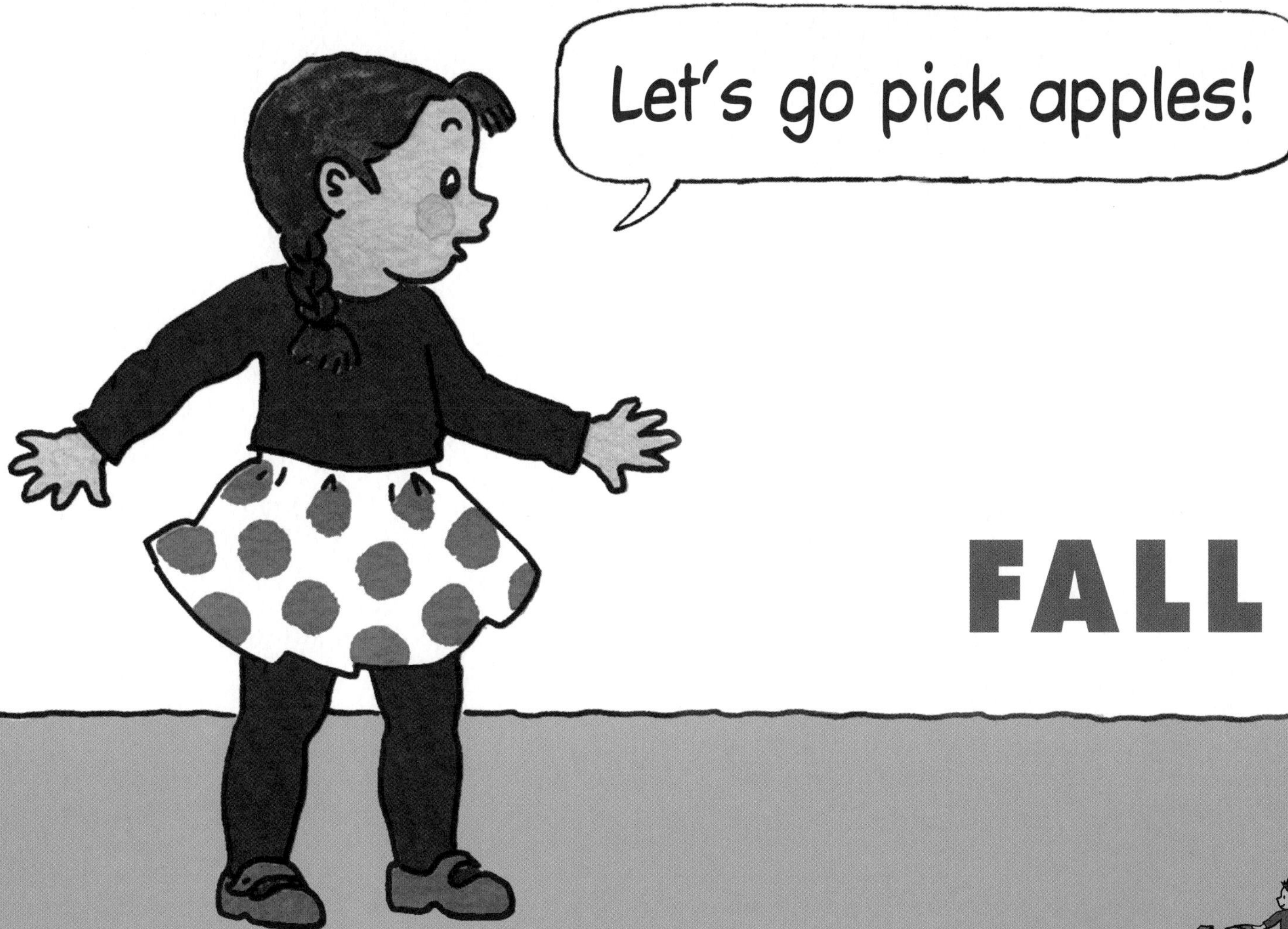
Let's go pick apples!

FALL

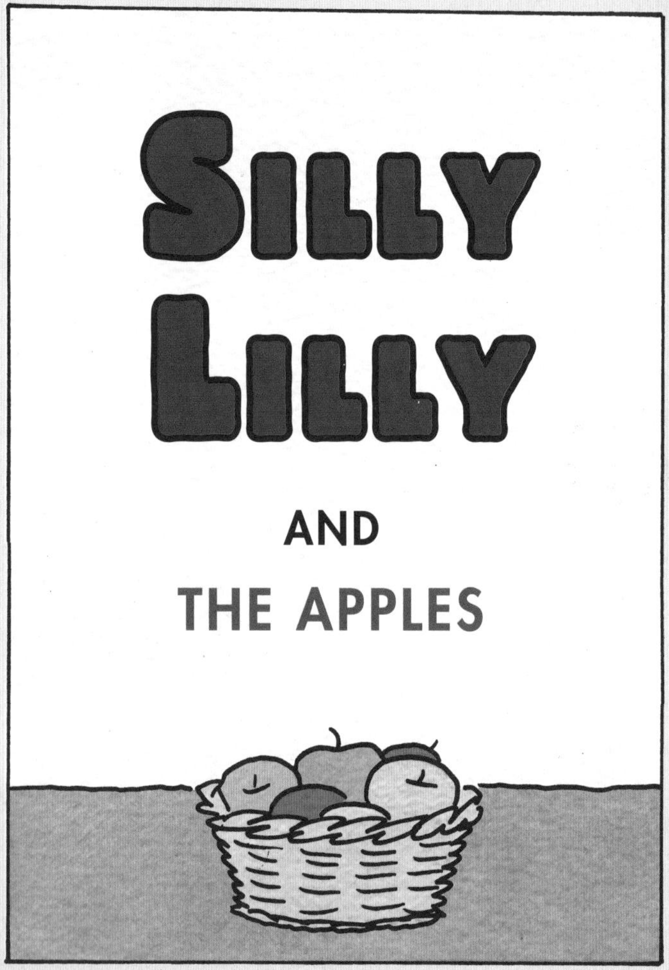
SILLY
LILLY
AND
THE APPLES

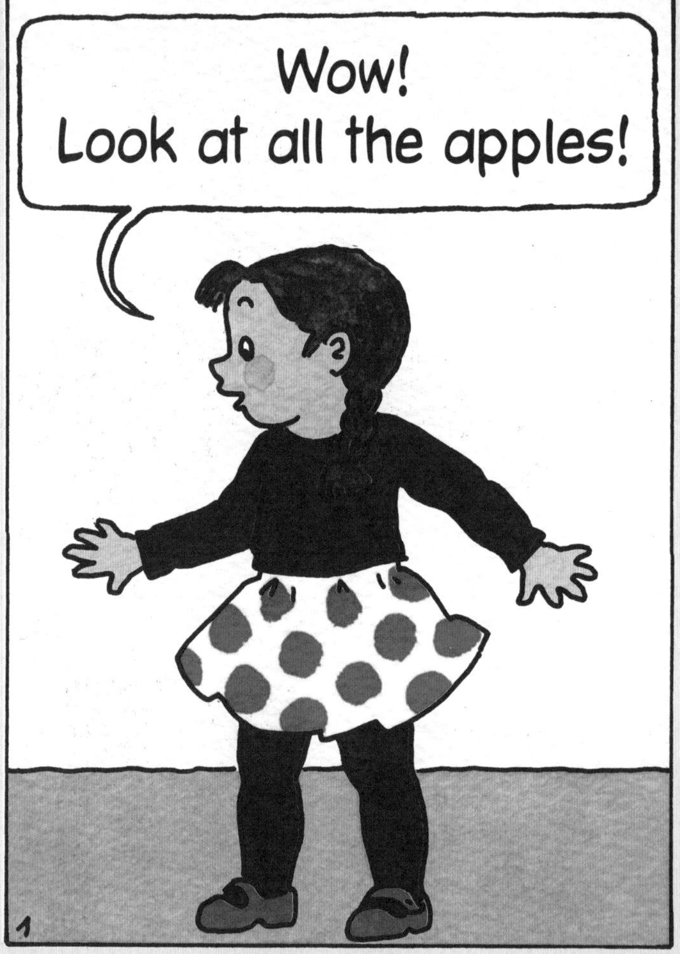
Wow!
Look at all the apples!
1

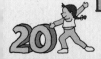

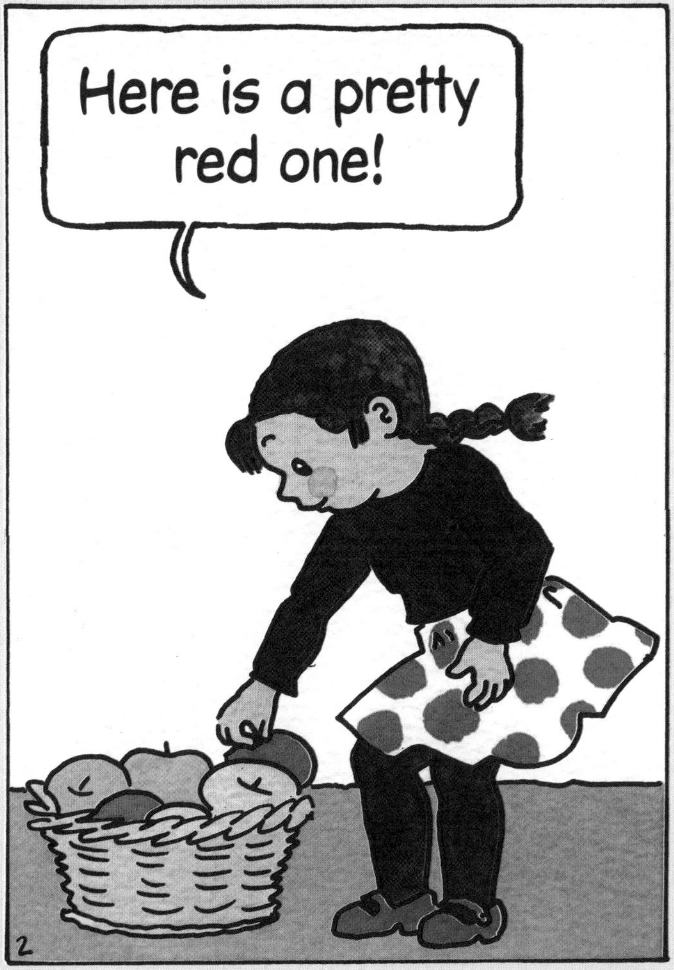
Here is a pretty red one!
2

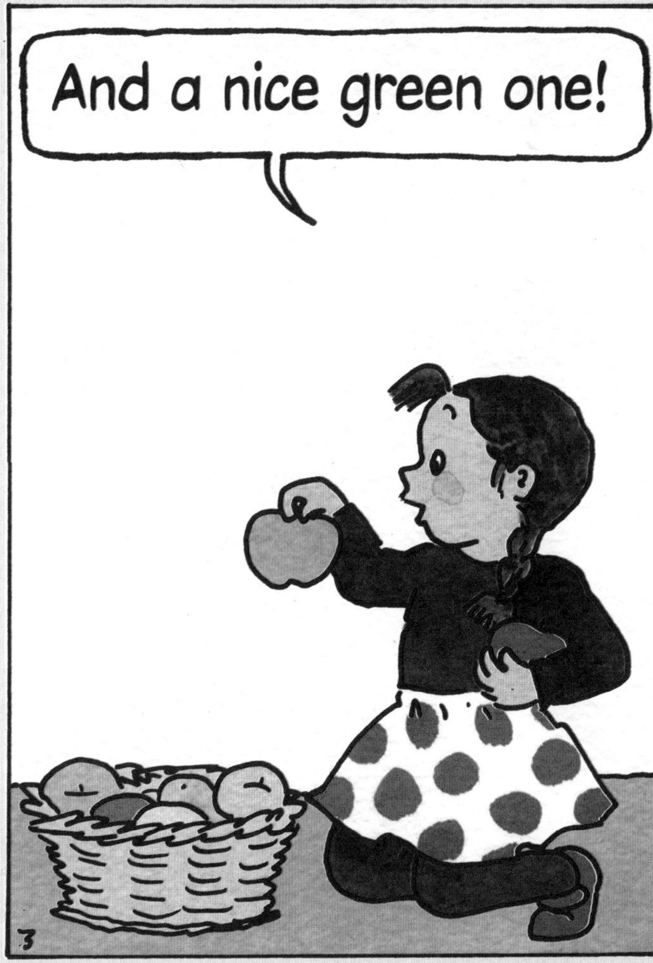
And a nice green one!
3

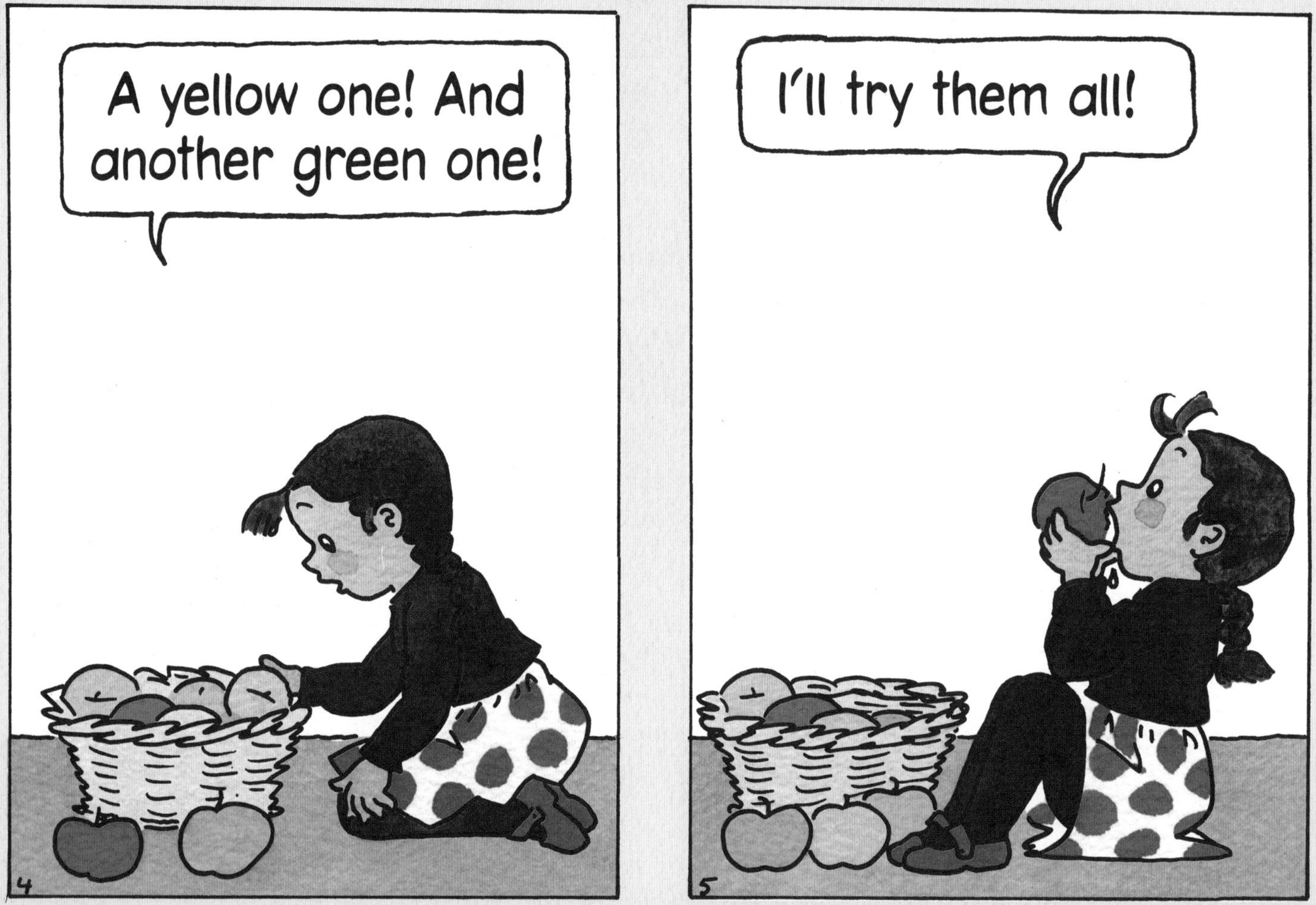
A yellow one! And another green one!
I'll try them all!

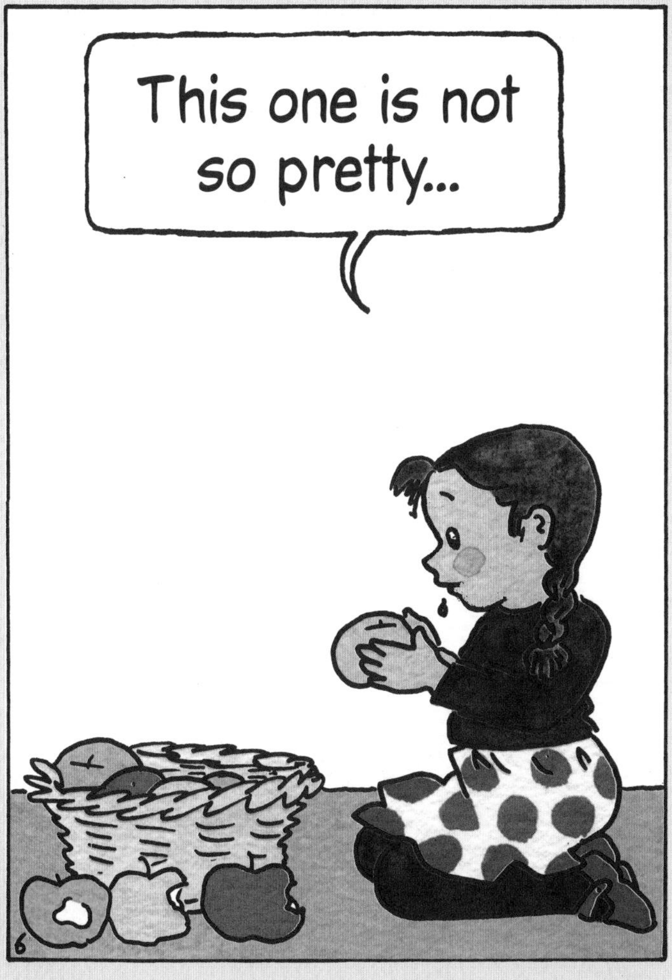
This one is not so pretty...

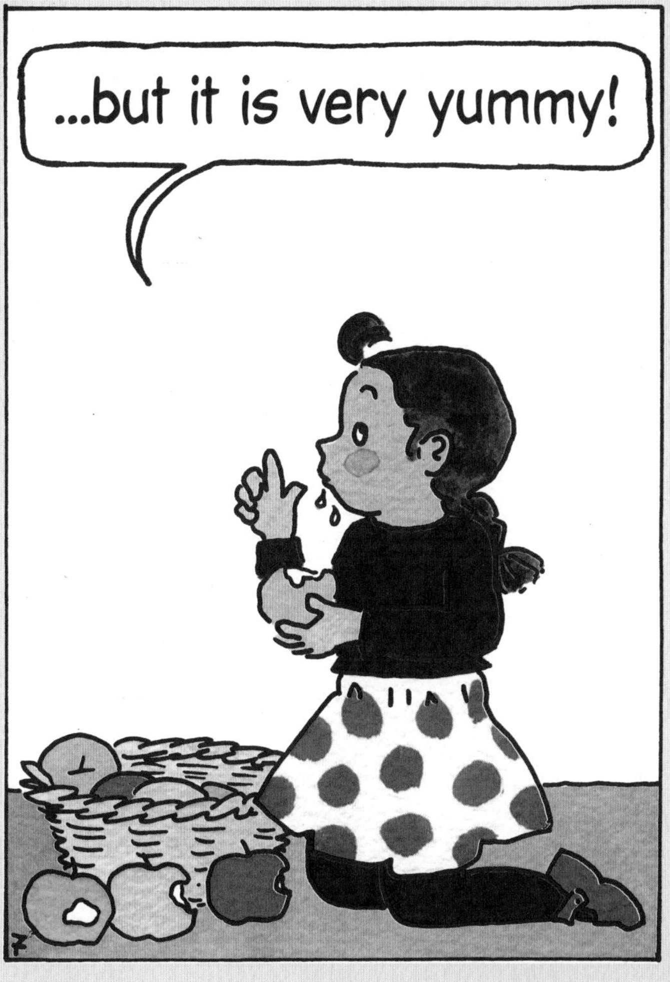
...but it is very yummy!

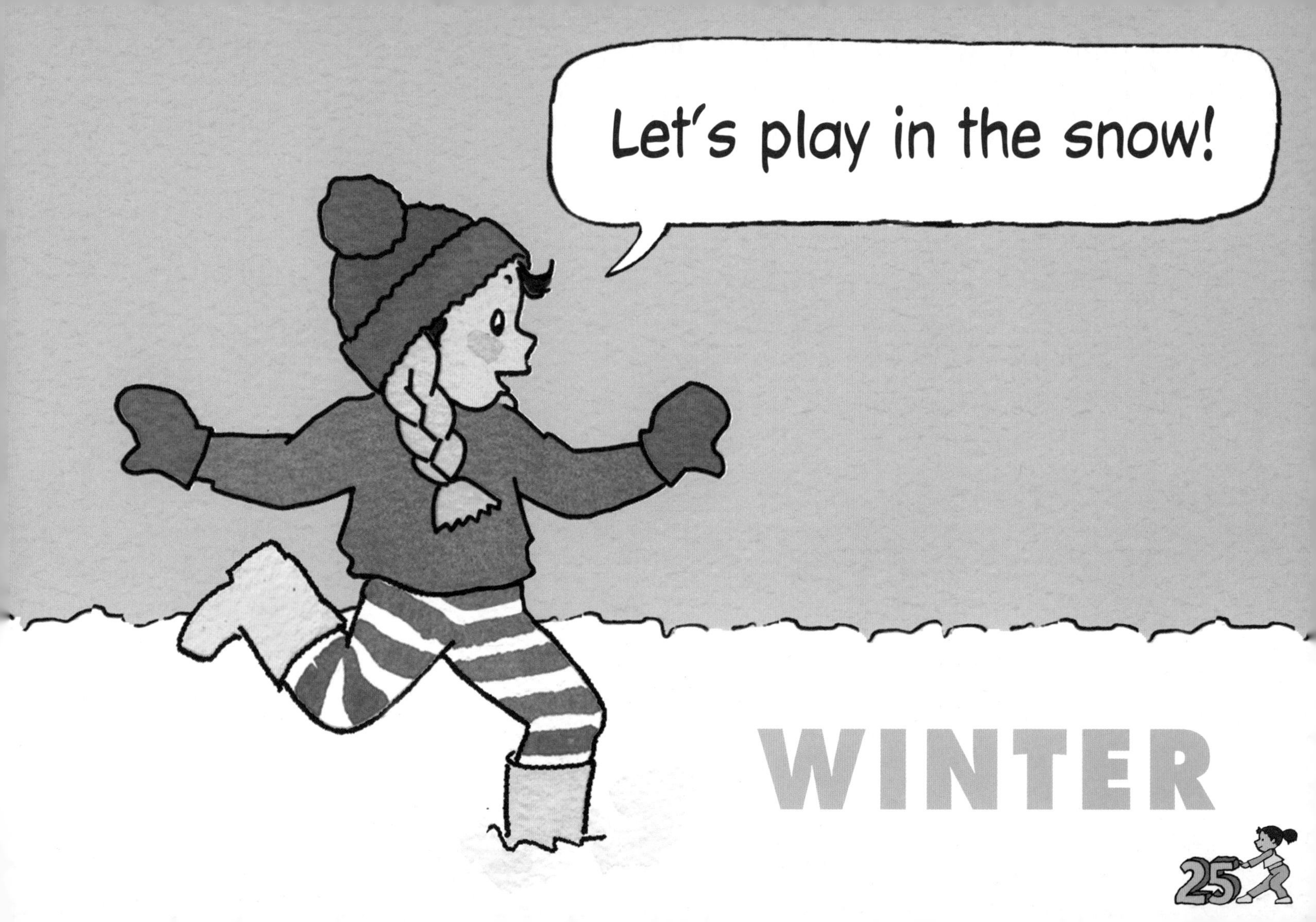
Let's play in the snow!
WINTER

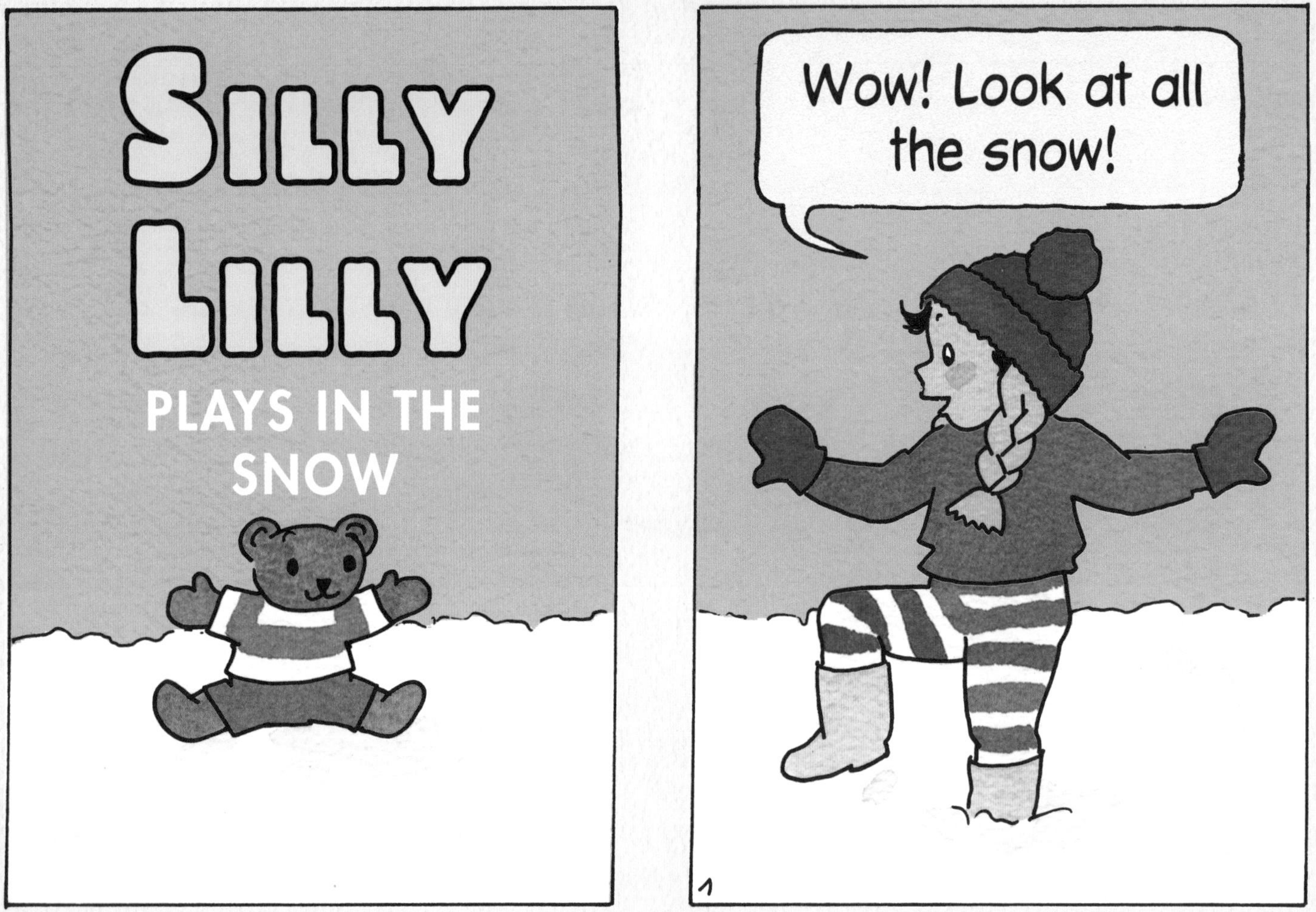
SILLY LILLY
PLAYS IN THE SNOW
Wow! Look at all the snow!
1

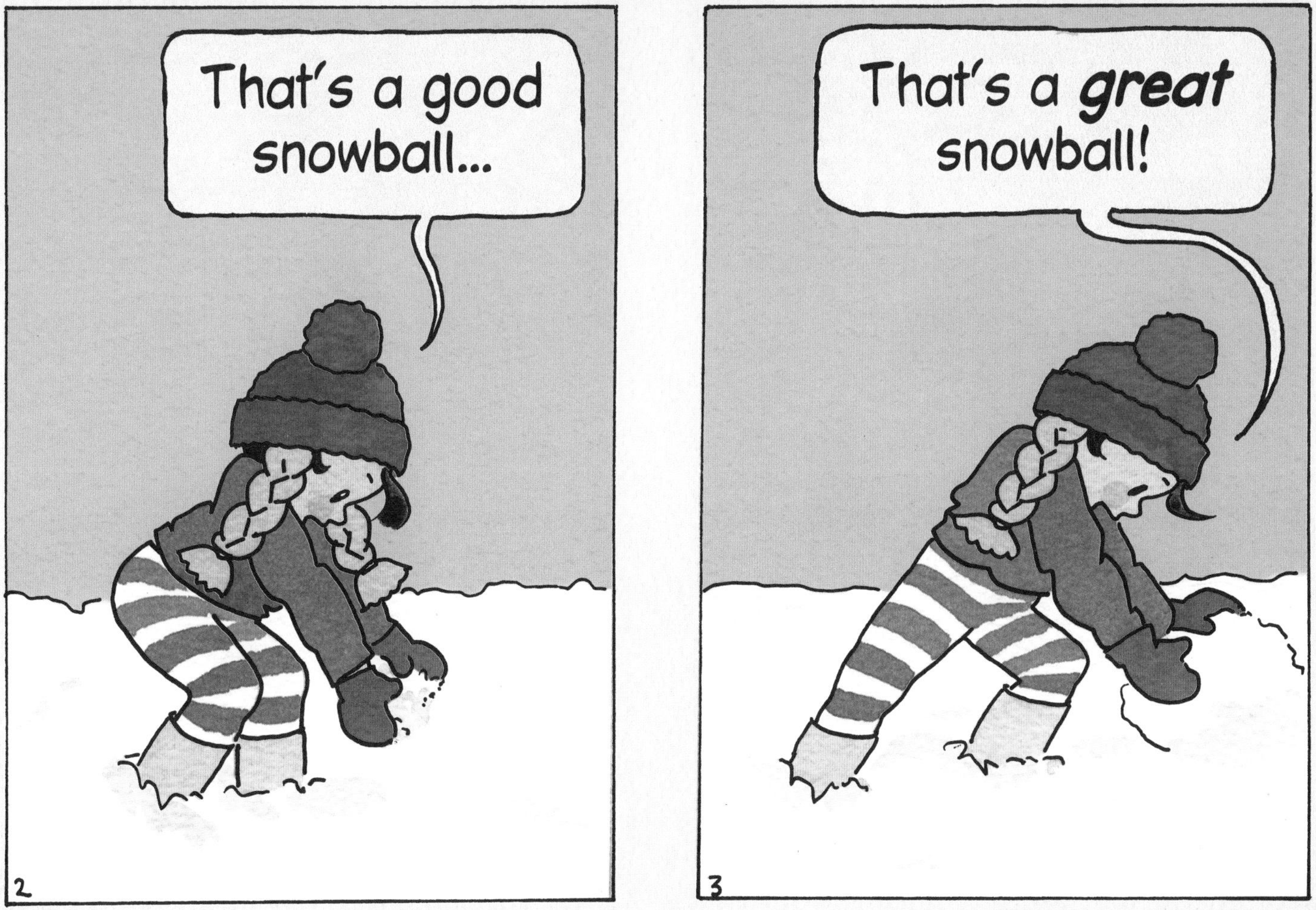
That's a good snowball...
2
That's a ***great*** snowball!
3

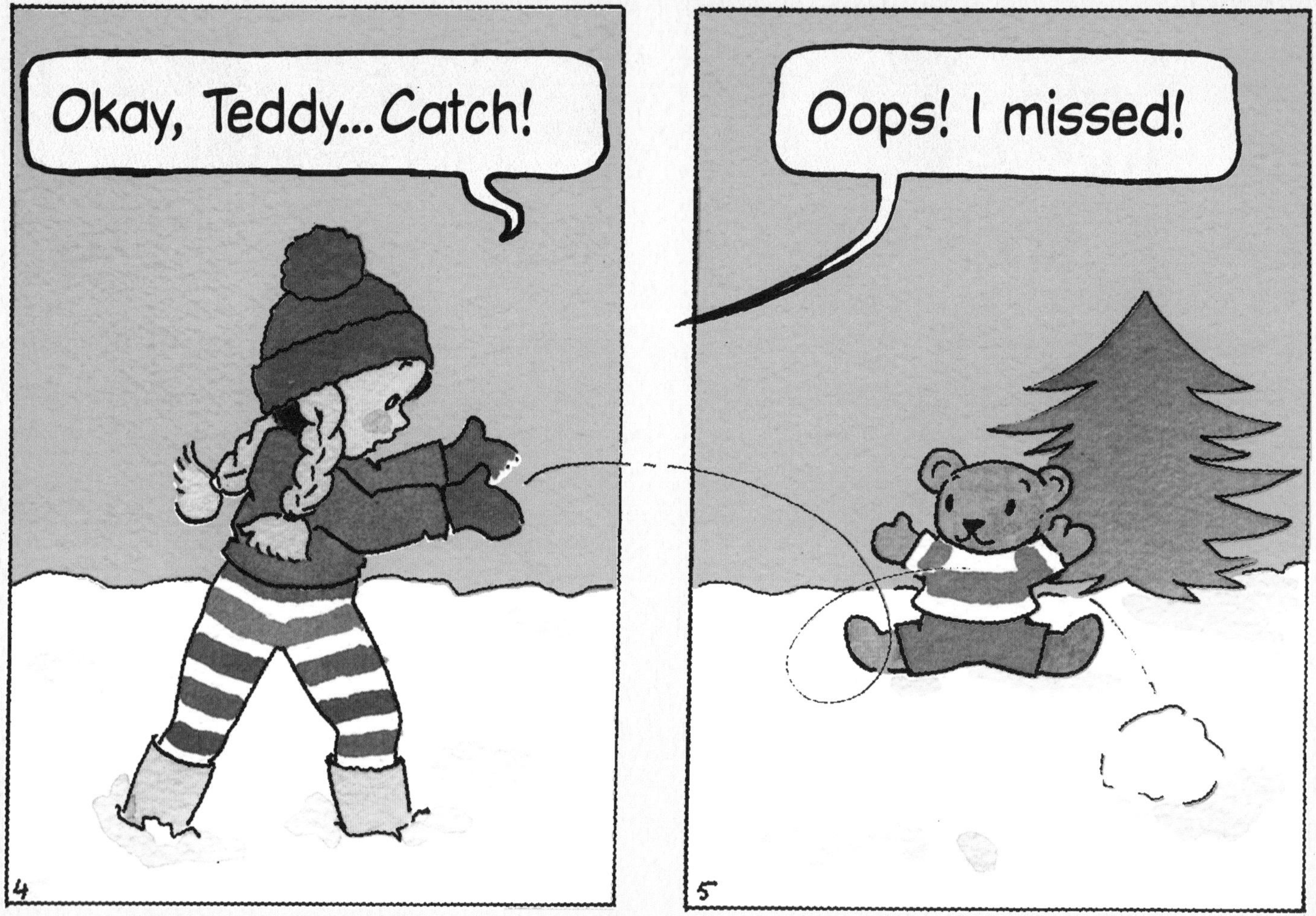
Okay, Teddy...Catch!
Oops! I missed!
4
5

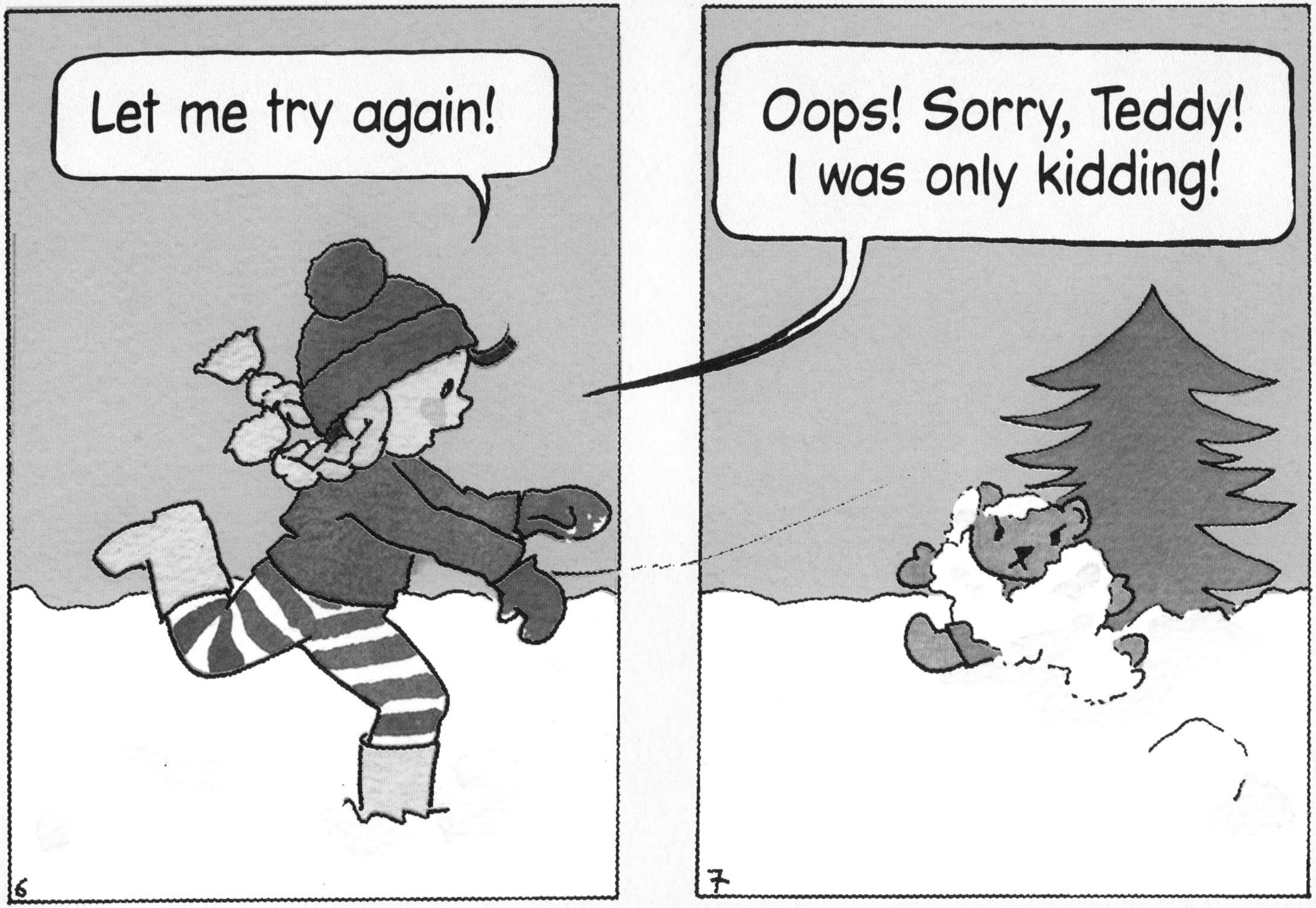
Let me try again!
Oops! Sorry, Teddy! I was only kidding!
6
7

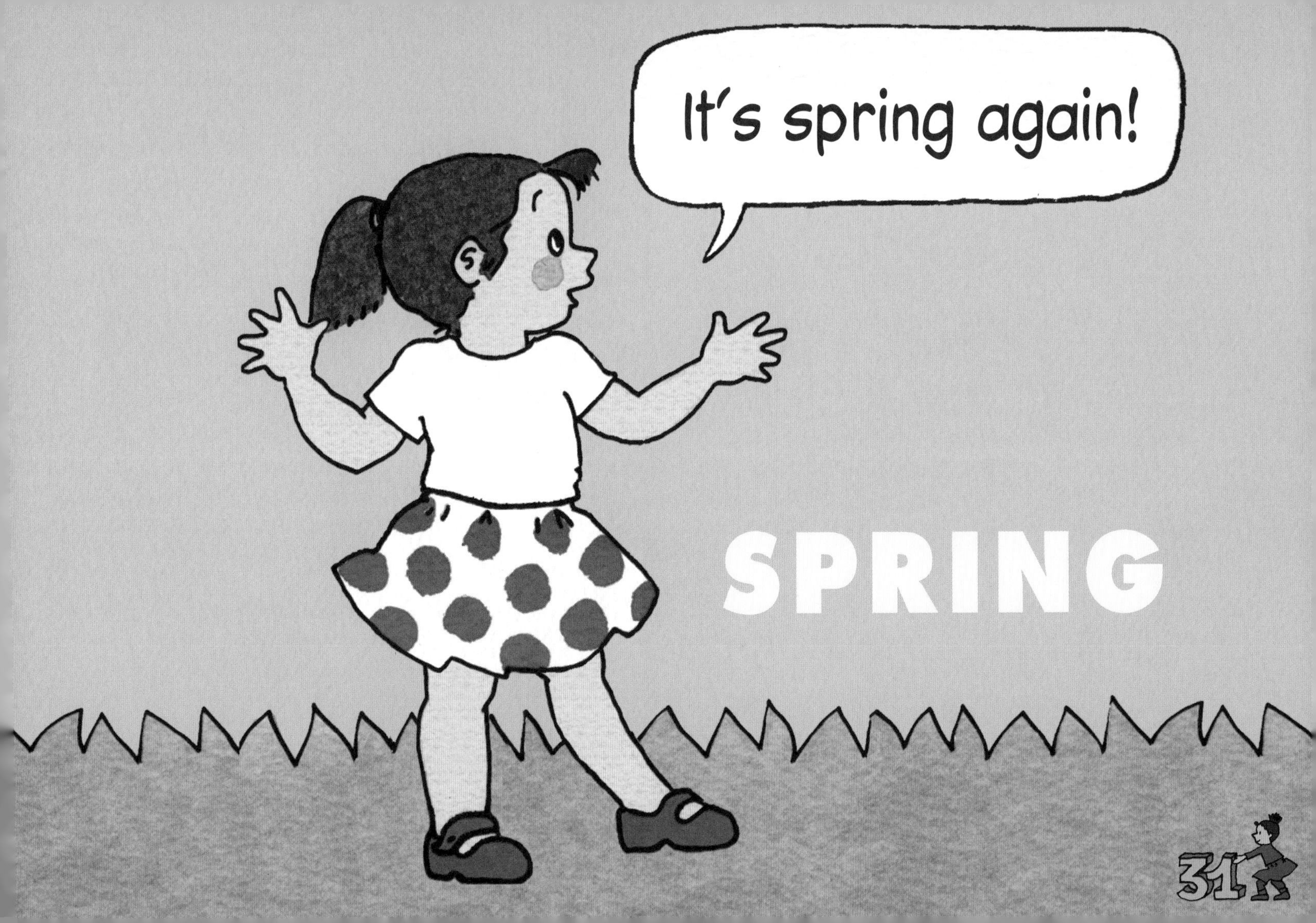
It's spring again!
SPRING

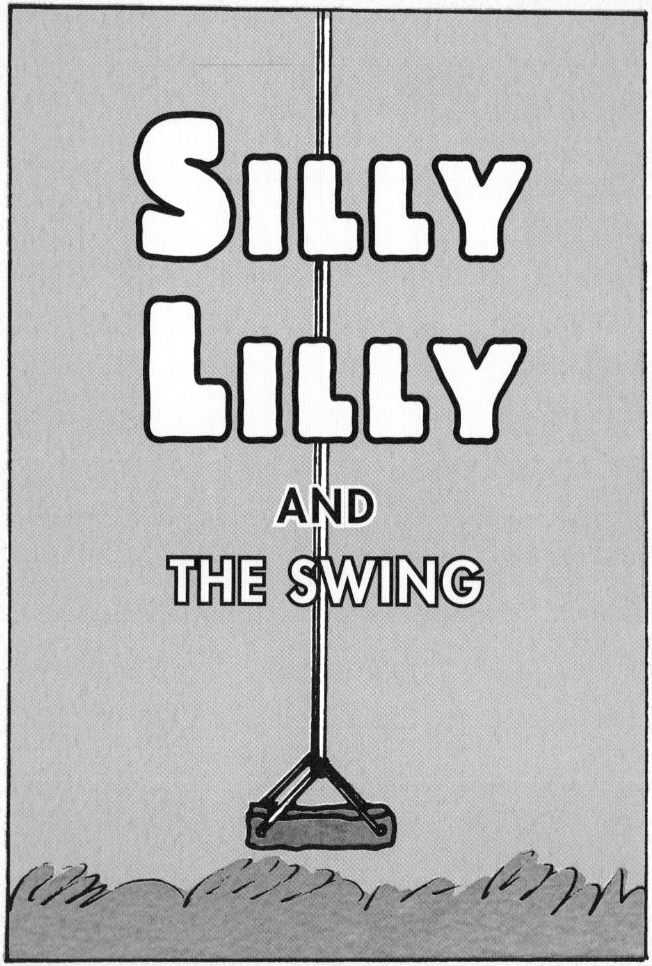
SILLY
LILLY
AND
THE SWING

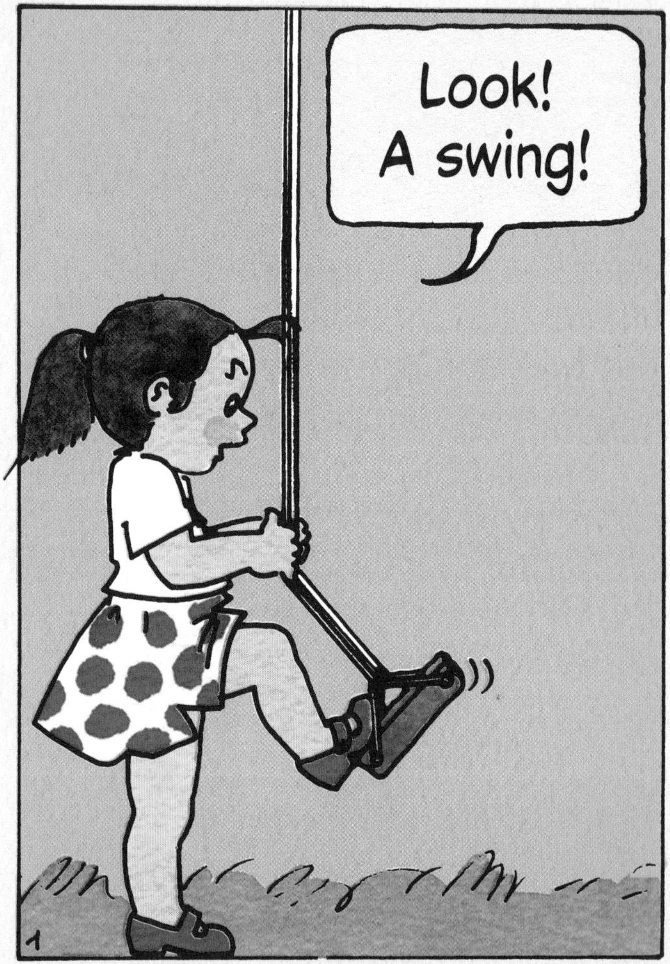
Look!
A swing!

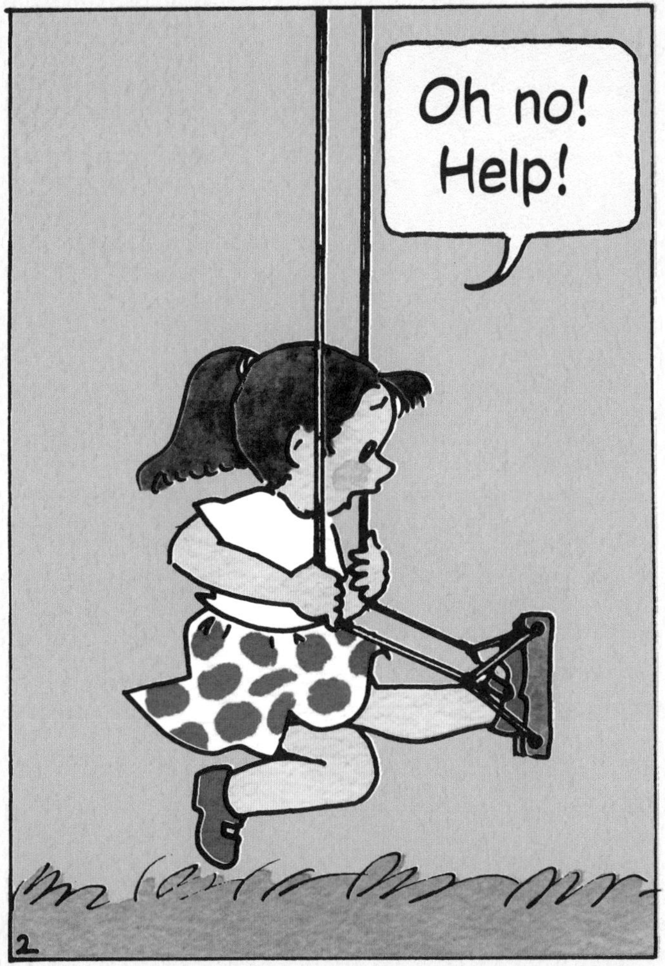
Oh no! Help!

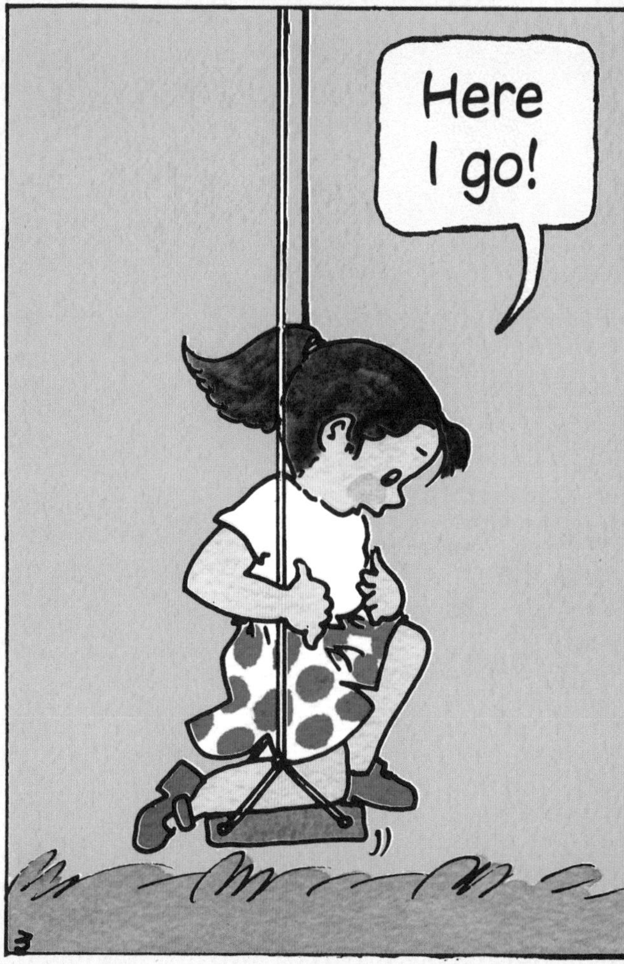
Here I go!

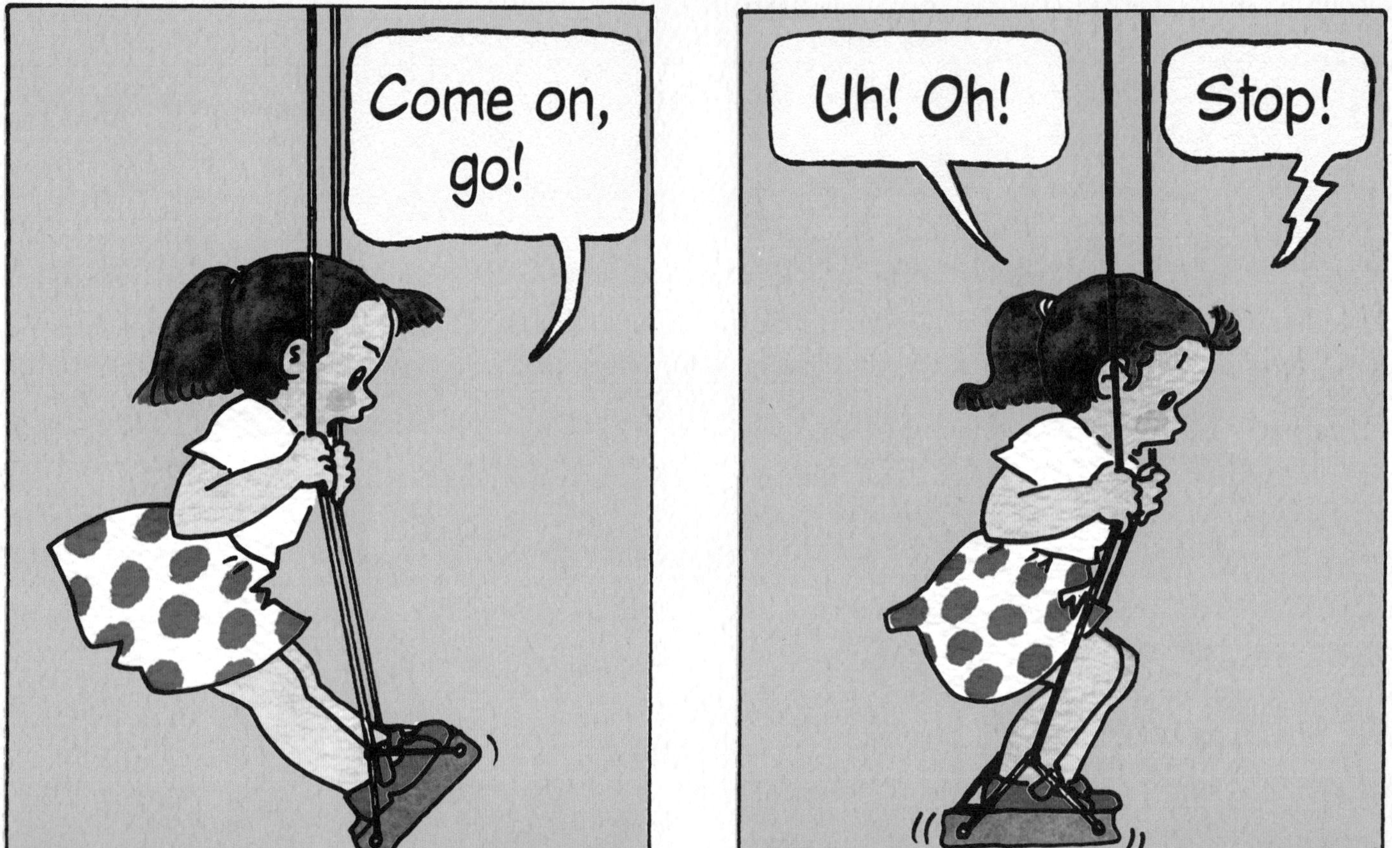
Come on, go!
4
Uh! Oh!
Stop!
5

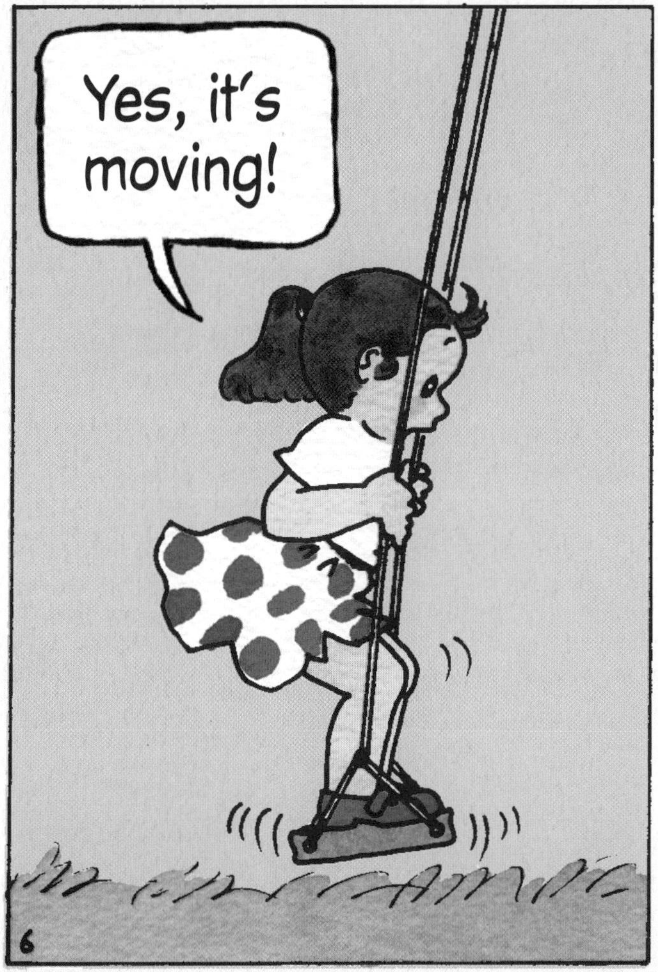
Yes, it's moving!
6

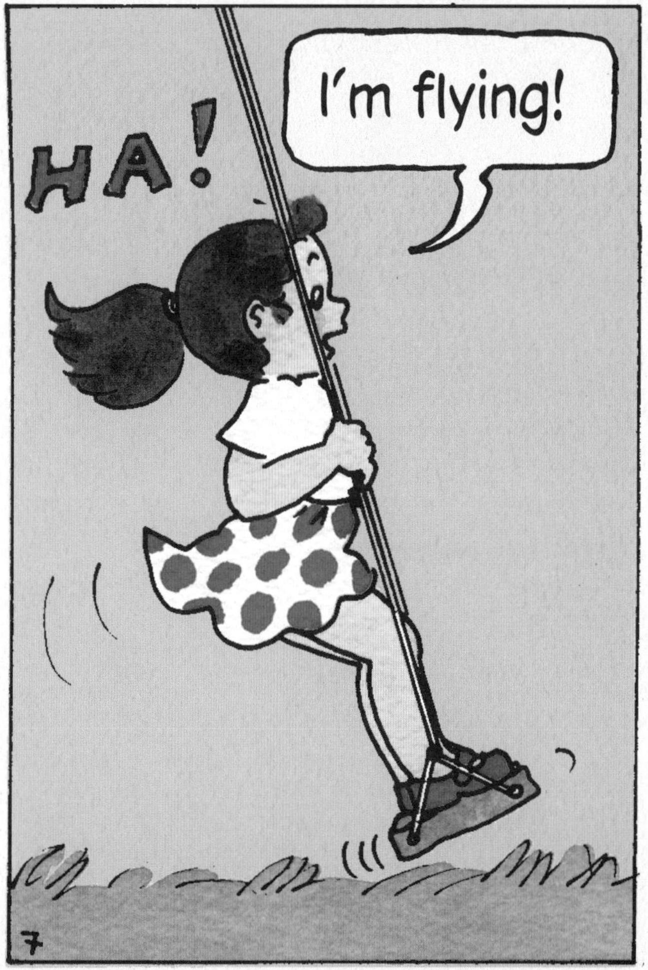
HA!
I'm flying!
7

HOW TO "TOON INTO READING"

in a few simple steps:

Our goal is to get kids reading—and we know kids LOVE comics. We publish award-winning early readers in comics form for elementary and early middle school, and present them in three levels.

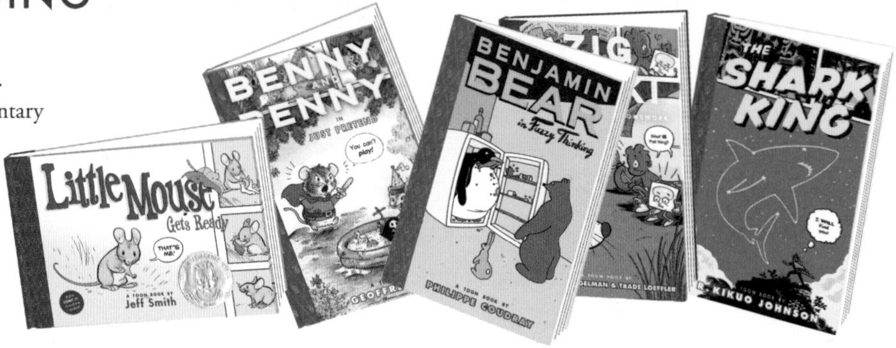

Little Mouse Gets Ready
THAT'S ME!
Jeff Smith
BENNY AND PENNY
IN JUST PRETEND
You can't play!
BENJAMIN BEAR in Fuzzy Thinking
A TOON BOOK BY
PHILIPPE COUDRAY
THE SHARK KING
R. KIKUO JOHNSON

1 FIND THE RIGHT BOOK

Veteran teacher Cindy Rosado tells what makes a good book for beginning and struggling readers alike: "A vetted vocabulary, plenty of picture clues, repetition, and a clear and compelling story. Also, the book shouldn't be too easy—or the reader won't learn, but neither should it be too hard—or he or she may get discouraged."

The **TOON INTO READING!™** program is designed for beginning readers and works wonders with reluctant readers.

2 GUIDE YOUNG READERS

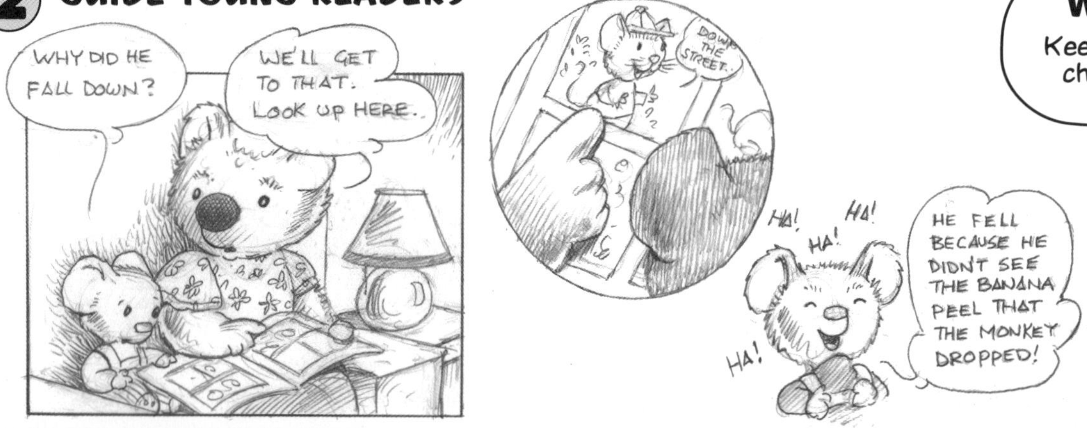

WHY DID HE FALL DOWN?
WE'LL GET TO THAT. LOOK UP HERE.
DOWN THE STREET.
HA! HA! HA! HA!
HE FELL BECAUSE HE DIDN'T SEE THE BANANA PEEL THAT THE MONKEY DROPPED!

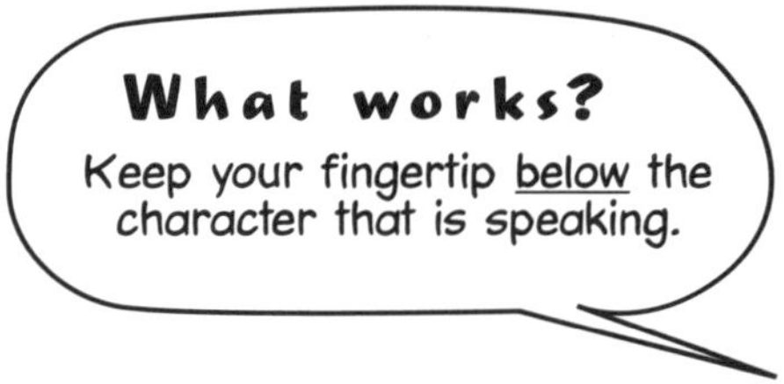

What works?
Keep your fingertip below the character that is speaking.

3 GET OUT THE CRAYONS

Kids see the hand of the author in a comic and it makes them want to tell their own stories. Encourage them to talk, write and draw!